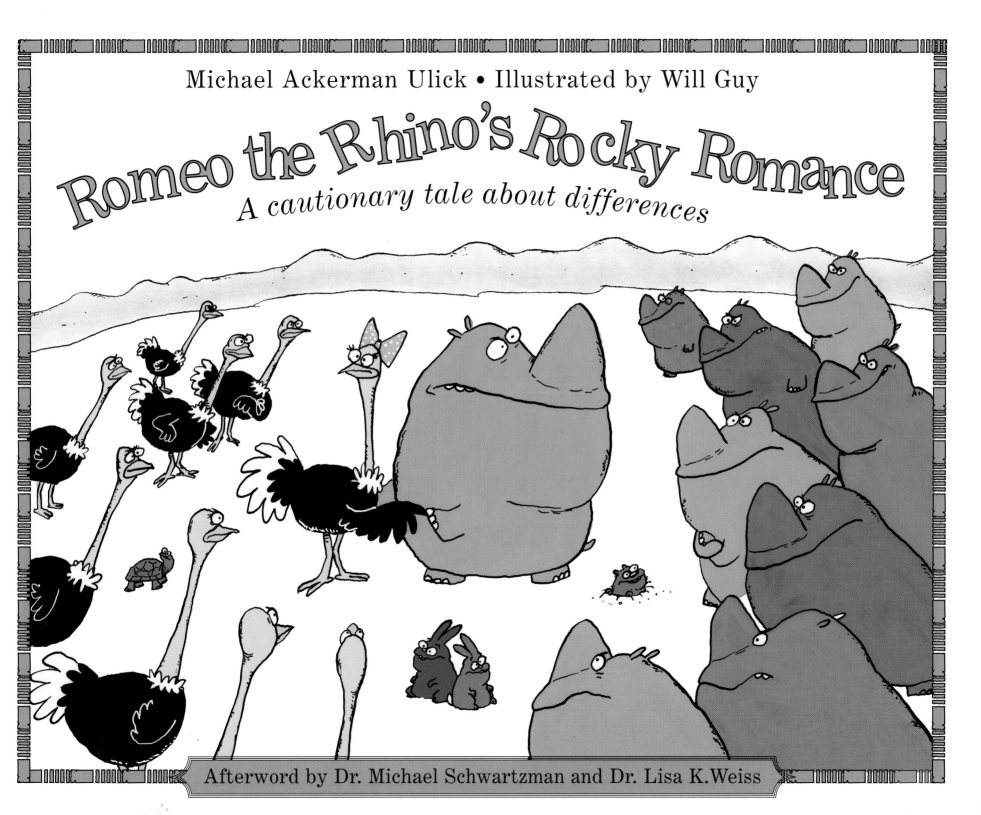

Michael Ackerman Ulick • Illustrated by Will Guy

Romeo the Rhino's Rocky Romance

A cautionary tale about differences

Afterword by Dr. Michael Schwartzman and Dr. Lisa K. Weiss

To Eddie, my muse.

Published by Footprints Press
Text copyright © 2000 Michael Ackerman Ulick
Illustrations copyright © 2000 Will Guy

Library of Congress PCN pfs 18729
ISBN: 0-9679813-0-1

Romeo the Rhino's Rocky Romance/Michael Ackerman Ulick

Summary: Romeo the Rhino and Astrid the Ostrich fall in love, much
to the dismay of the other rhinos and ostriches. This is a story about
discrimination and how Romeo is able to overcome it. An afterword
written by child psychologists, Drs. Schwartzman and Weiss, follows.

[1. Adventure - fiction 2. Moral values - fiction
3. Discrimination/Differences - fiction 4. Animal stories - fiction]

Book design by Fearn Cutler
Printed in Hong Kong by South China Printing Co. (1988) LTD

The bright, yellow heat from the afternoon sun made Romeo the Rhino thirsty.

He waddled over to the watering hole
where a flock of ostriches were drinking.
One of them looked up and shouted, "Go away,
you big, clumsy rhinoceros! This is our spot."

"Why can't I drink here?" asked Romeo. "The watering hole is for all the animals."

"Because this side is for beautiful birds, not ugly rhinos," cackled the ostrich. "Stay in the mud with your own kind."

Why were they
always nasty to
rhinoceroses?
Just because
Romeo was different
from the ostriches didn't
mean they were any better than he was.
Romeo's feelings were very hurt.

He backed away and bumped into something. "Excuse me," apologized Romeo. Astrid the Ostrich smiled back, shyly, "Oh, that's alright."

Romeo's heart went THUMP!
She was the most beautiful bird he had ever seen.

Astrid whispered to her sister Agnes,
"Don't you think he's attractive…in a
triceratops sort of way?" Agnes shook
her head. "You have strange taste, little sister."
"But his ears are so cute," giggled Astrid.

Agnes became impatient. "We are graceful birds that can run like the wind. How can you find such an ugly creature cute?" And she quickly shoved Astrid toward the other ostriches.

His nose was huge.

Romeo looked at his reflection
in the water. He certainly
was no movie star.

His legs were stubby

His skin was leathery.

And for such a large animal his
tail was ridiculously small.

But Romeo had good qualities. He was brave and strong. And he cared about all the animals, especially Astrid.

"I will serenade her tonight and win her heart," he thought.

ROMEO'S VIRTUES

The soft breezes
filled the night air
with romance. Romeo
stood under Astrid's
balcony and sang
Neapolitan love songs.
Astrid peeked coyly from
behind her shutters, listening.
He had such a lovely tenor's voice.

"Go sing somewhere else,
you big oaf!" shouted Astrid's
mother and father. And without
warning they slammed the doors shut.

Poor Romeo. His heart felt very heavy inside his chest. They would never allow him to court Astrid. Ostriches and rhinos just didn't mix.

He spent the rest of the night sitting
in a pool of tears.

The morning sun rose.

Romeo had barely slept a wink. Rubbing his red eyes
he noticed something unusual.

A jeep and a big truck were racing
towards Astrid's village.

"They're after ostrich feathers. They use them to decorate ladies' hats. We must save the ostriches!"

"Hold on!" Rollo the elder spoke. "Rhinos, not ostriches are an endangered species. And besides, our horns are far more valuable than a bunch of their feathers. If those hunters discover us their greedy eyes will see even bigger dollar signs."

"But we all live together," pleaded Romeo. "We should help one another. Remember our motto…"

"Not when it concerns the ostriches," warned Rollo. "They're just a flock of wimpy snobs!"

There was no time to waste. Astrid was in grave danger.
All alone, Romeo charged down the hill.

Faster and faster he ran.
His hoof-beats sounded like rolling thunder.

One of the hunters spun around and saw a gathering cloud of dust.

He screamed , "TORNADO!" and drove away in the jeep. The others were frozen in terror. Astrid's parents, expecting the worst, stuck their heads in the sand.

As the huge cloud was almost upon them, Romeo broke out into daylight.
He was headed straight for the truck.

BAM!
Romeo rammed it with his horn.

The hunters were caught off guard and scattered. Once again Romeo's powerful legs flew him toward the truck.

BOOM! The truck went sailing high into the air. A minute later, there was not a hunter in sight. They had run away never to return.

All the animals watched this amazing spectacle. The ostriches circled around Romeo hailing him as their great hero. "Hurray!" they cheered. "Romeo saved us!" The other rhinos joined in the celebration.

That night there was a big party in Romeo's honor. Rhinos and ostriches mixed together and learned that they had much in common. They also realized their differences could make life at the watering hole much more interesting.

Romeo and Astrid held hands and gazed at the crescent moon above the plain. Just as they were about to hug, Astrid's mother tip-toed over. "Romeo," she said, "Would you mind if I stroke your little ears? They're so cute!"

Romeo the Rhino's Rocky Romance: AFTERWORD

When your child comes home from school and talks about a painful experience involving discrimination, what can you do? How should you respond when he is insensitive and hurtful towards another child? During these upsetting times, whether your child is feeling badly or showing a lack of empathy, *Romeo the Rhino* offers a constructive framework to help you sort it out together.

Kids can experience and communicate prejudice and exclusion at an early age. They realize that there are differences among people. But when those differences are negatively perceived, discrimination and insensitivity can have an ugly influence on your child's character development. Whether your child is called "four eyes" or some racial epithet, he can identify with Romeo and how it felt when the ostriches called him a "big, clumsy rhinocerous." And if your child is the one calling names, he can learn a lesson from the experiences of the clannish, intolerant ostriches.

But what can you do as a parent to help your child in these situations? First, it is most important to let your child tell you, in his own words, what happened. Listen and try to understand his point of view. Then, try to understand the situation from the other child's perspective. It is essential that you put aside your own emotions. Next, reassure your child by letting him know that you understand why he is so upset. If he spoke in a derogatory way, explain why the other child would feel so badly. Your admonishment should focus on encouraging him to change his behavior, rather than to punish. Drawing parallels between his experiences and those of the characters in *Romeo the Rhino* are simple ways to get at some of those feelings.

The final moments of *Romeo the Rhino* help round out the story. Romeo and Astrid are drawn to each other by their differences—*opposites attract.* Their relationship benefits all the animals by helping them develop a sense of tolerance and acceptance. This introduces the final theme of the story—caring and belonging within a larger community, the value of diversity. Romeo explains, "We all live together. We should help each other." As the animals get to know each other, they learn to appreciate their differences. Prejudice and exclusion are replaced by understanding, empathy and caring, and all the animals can live together in harmony.

Dr. Michael Schwartzman
Dr. Lisa K. Weiss